Wolfmen Don't
Hula Dance

There are more books about the Bailey School Kids!
Have you read these adventures?

Wolfmen Don't Hula Dance

by Debbie Dadey
and
Marcia Thornton Jones

illustrated by John Steven Gurney

A
LITTLE APPLE
PAPERBACK

SCHOLASTIC INC.
New York Toronto London Auckland Sydney
Mexico City New Delhi Hong Kong

To Jake Spector and all his "howling"
good ideas! — MTJ and DD

ISBN 0-590-18986-7

12 11 10 9 8 7 6 5 4   1 2 3 4/0

Printed in the U.S.A.   40

First Scholastic printing, May 1999

Contents

1

Luau

"This will be the worst weekend of the entire third grade," Eddie griped. He was following his three friends Howie, Melody, and Liza down the school hallway toward the gym. Each of them carried a huge bundle of paper flowers they'd made for the annual Bailey School dinner. All the classes were making decorations and taking them to the gym, where a group of parents would load them on buses later in the afternoon.

"I think a luau is a great idea," Liza said, sticking a flower in her blond hair. "We get to wear flowers and eat around a campfire."

"I'd rather burn these flowers than wear them," Eddie told her. He shook his bundle until one of the paper petals

1

floated onto his freckled nose. "The whole idea is stupid."

"There's one good thing about it," Howie said. "We get to eat outside."

"That's right," Melody said. "Last year everybody had to wear dress-up clothes and use their best manners. This year, we all get to go to Camp Lone Wolf and cook food over a fire."

"I just hope there aren't any wolves there," Liza said with a shudder. They all remembered their hairy camp director, Mr. Jenkins. They were sure he was a werewolf ready to eat them for dinner the last time they were at Camp Lone Wolf.

"We have nothing to worry about," Melody hurried to say. "Plenty of parents are going, and Mrs. Jeepers will be there."

"Mrs. Jeepers is worse than a pack of starving werewolves," Eddie said.

The kids were quiet as they thought about their teacher. Most third-graders believed Mrs. Jeepers was a vampire and that the green brooch she wore was full of magic that made kids like Eddie behave.

"We never proved Mrs. Jeepers was a vampire," Melody said. "Besides, your grandmother is on the luau committee. She won't let anything bad happen."

"Melody's right," Howie said finally. "A luau at Camp Lone Wolf is a great idea for the annual dinner."

"Maybe it won't be bad," Eddie said as they neared the gym door. "But the report we have to do on Hawaii for Monday is bound to kill me!"

"A little homework won't hurt you," Howie said.

"Besides, it'll be interesting learning about Hawaii," Liza added.

"Not as interesting as playing soccer," Eddie told them as he pulled open the gym door.

Just as Eddie opened the door, Liza gasped. "What happened to the gym?"

4

2

Hula

Ten torches made flickering shadows on the stage at the far end of the gym. Kindergartners were sprawled on the floor, staring up at a group of beautiful dancers wearing long grass skirts. Behind them, men beat a rumbling rhythm on drums, shook rattles, and chanted strange words. The dancers stepped to the rhythm. They waved their hands and wiggled their bodies so the grass skirts swished in crazy patterns.

"Those must be the hula dancers for tomorrow's luau," Liza said.

"Oh, great," Eddie mumbled. "Not only do I have to do homework, but I have to watch a bunch of sissy dancers, too."

"That guy doesn't look like a sissy," Melody said and pointed at the stage.

A huge man had jumped from behind the curtain, scattering the women dancers in the grass skirts. His eyes were a pale yellow that made the kids shiver.

"Look at the muscles on that dancer," Melody said. "He must be the strongest man in all of Hawaii."

"Who cares?" Eddie said. "All he does is dance. Let's go."

"I want to stay and watch for a while," Liza said. "There's something very interesting about their dance. It's like they're telling a story."

"Dancing is for girls," Eddie told them.

"You'd better not let that hula guy hear you," Melody pointed out. "He could lift you up with one finger!"

"He's definitely strong," Howie said.

"And hairy," Liza added. It was true. The hula guy had long black hair and a short beard that grew so far up on his cheeks it almost reached his eyes. His eyebrows were so bushy they met over his nose. He even wore a grass skirt and

6

a huge belt that was made of brown-and-black hair tied around his waist. Liza was sure she even saw hair growing on top of his feet.

"He should be careful," Eddie said with a laugh. "With all that hair, he might be asked to dance at a ball — the hair ball!"

Eddie stopped laughing when the chanting grew louder and the drummers' rhythm became fast and frantic. All at once, the music stopped. The gym seemed to echo with the sudden silence.

One of the other dancers grabbed the hairy belt and pulled it from the hula guy's waist. When she did, he let out a bloodcurdling howl. Then he grabbed a flaming torch and held it high over his head. Liza couldn't help but notice that his eyes glowed red in the firelight.

Then, without even blinking, the hula guy swallowed the fire.

3

Legend

"We can't leave now," Eddie hissed. "It's just getting good. Maybe he'll teach me how to eat fire."

"We have to go," Howie said, pulling Eddie from the gym. "We need to do research for our report about Hawaii."

"You always know how to spoil a good time," Eddie griped. But he followed Howie, Liza, and Melody to the school's library.

As soon as they got there, Howie used the computer to look up a book about Hawaiian folklore. Melody looked in the encyclopedia to learn about Hawaii's plants and animals. Liza searched the shelves for a book about hula dancing. Eddie didn't care about any of that stuff.

He wanted to find a book about fire eating.

They piled their books on a table and sat down to read. "Aren't they beautiful?" Liza said, pointing to a picture of hula dancers. "They look just like the dancers in the gym."

"Maybe we could learn how to hula dance," Melody suggested.

"Dancing is stupid," Eddie said. "All you do is wiggle your body. What's so hard about that?" Eddie stood up and wiggled his behind until the librarian glared at him. He slid into his seat and acted like he was reading until she looked away.

"Dancing the hula isn't that easy," Liza said. "According to this book, all the body movements of hula dancing are meant to tell a story."

"The only stories I'm interested in are about monsters and soccer," Eddie told her. "The last thing I want to hear is a story about dancing."

Liza showed Eddie a picture in her book. "But there are hula stories about warriors and chiefs," she said. "The dances also tell about the beauty of the land, and they can tell about love."

"Yuck," Eddie said. "The only thing I love is death and destruction!"

"Then you would like the hula about the monster from ancient Hawaiian folklore," Liza told Eddie. "That hula has something to do with a hairy beast that appeared suddenly, wreaking death and destruction in a remote Hawaiian village near a famous volcano."

"That's impossible," Melody said. "According to the encyclopedia, there were no animals like that in Hawaii."

Just then, Howie looked up from reading his book. His face was pale and his voice shook when he spoke. "According to my book," he said, "there is a little-known legend about a beast that terrorized a village. The villagers finally saved themselves by chasing the beast

with flaming torches straight into the mouth of an erupting volcano. The beast was never seen again, but on nights when the sky glows with the light of the moon, a lonely howl can sometimes be heard coming from the steep cliffs of the volcano."

"What did the beast look like?" Melody asked.

"It looked exactly like it was part man and part wolf," Howie said. "A wolfman."

Howie held up the book so his friends could see the picture. Liza took one look at the picture and shrieked, "Oh, no!"

"Shhhh, be quiet," Melody warned. "Before we get in trouble."

"But don't you see?" Liza asked. "The dance we saw in the gym must be about this rare legend. What if," she said slowly, "that dancer is really the legendary wolf-man?"

4

Wolfman

"He was hairy," Howie said slowly.

"That was just a furry belt," Eddie told them.

"What about his beard?" Liza said. "I've never met anybody with eyebrows that bushy, and I know I saw hair on his toes."

"You have hair growing on your eyeballs," Eddie said. "After all, wolfmen don't hula dance."

"Eddie's right," Melody said. "Besides, there is no such thing as a wolfman, especially in a paradise like Hawaii."

"Don't be so sure," Howie said. "I've read about this. Wolfmen have been spotted in Scandinavia, England, Germany, and France. That shows they're able to travel great distances. There is nothing

15

to stop a wolfman from traveling to Hawaii."

"The only way he could get there," Eddie said with a giggle, "would be to dog-paddle!"

"That's not true," Howie said, ignoring Eddie's joke. "Nobody lived on Hawaii to begin with. The first people got there by rowing boats. A wolfman could take a boat just as easily as anybody else. There is a way to find out."

"How?" Melody asked.

Howie didn't answer. Instead, he got up and hurried to the shelves. He quickly found the book he was looking for and came back to his chair. "This," he said, "has all the answers." He held up a book called *Creatures of the Night*.

"See what it says about wolfmen," Liza suggested. "Maybe we'll find proof that the hula guy really is a wolfman."

"Or we might find proof that Liza's brain was fried by the sun," Eddie joked.

Howie used the index to quickly flip to

the page he needed. "'The horrible wolf-man wears a belt made from the fur of a wolf tied around his waist,'" Howie read. "'The belt is believed to give a mortal man the power to change into a mighty beast that is part man and part wolf. When a normal man puts on the magic wolf belt in the black of night, he turns into a murderous monster who can only think of one thing — eating raw meat.'"

"It's true," Liza whimpered. "The hula guy was wearing a fur belt. He must be a wolfman."

"Then why wasn't he a monster instead of a sissy dancer?" Eddie asked her.

"I think I can answer that," Howie interrupted. "'Only two things could protect a mortal from the magic of the belt,'" he read from his book. "'The bright light of day is known to melt its magic, and that is why a wolfman is never seen during the day. It also explains why wolfmen are afraid of bright light, for it will melt their power, leaving them powerless during their bloodthirsty hunt.'"

"So the hula dancer couldn't turn into a wolfman because it's daylight," Melody said.

Liza shivered. "Remember how he howled? Do you think wolfmen howl at the people they want to eat?"

"No," Eddie joked, "they shake salt and pepper on the people they want to eat."

"That's it!" Melody squealed. "I know how we can get rid of the wolfman. We'll make him eat some of Howie's garlic potato chips. They have lots of salt."

"Don't you remember anything I've taught you about monsters?" Howie groaned. "Salt cures zombies, not wolfmen."

"Then what cures a wolfman?" Liza asked.

Howie looked at his book. "According to this, wolfmen are deathly afraid of water. Some people believe that water breaks the curse of the belt."

"Great," Melody said. "We're getting ready to go to a luau with a bloodthirsty wolfman and the only protection we'll have is a water gun."

"What if water doesn't work?" Liza asked.

Howie gulped. "Then we'll end up as wolfman sandwiches."

5

Stinkers

"Let's make a club," Eddie suggested on the way to the luau the next afternoon. The kids were piled in the back of Eddie's grandmother's van.

Liza smiled from the backseat of the van. "Good," Liza said, "I love clubs. Can I help make the rules?"

Eddie shook his head. "There's only one rule. Everybody in the club must hate Hawaiian dancing. It's the 'I Hate Luaus Club.'"

Melody folded her arms over her chest. "That's not a very nice club," she said. "Besides, you're already in a club."

"What's that?" Eddie asked.

Melody giggled. "You're the president of the Stinkers of America Club."

Howie laughed. "I always knew Eddie would be president of something."

Eddie started to complain, but his grandmother interrupted. "Here we are," she said, turning down a gravel driveway. The van bounced over a big bump and went under a huge banner that read BAILEY SCHOOL LUAU.

Mr. Jenkins, the camp director, waved them into a parking space. His hair was so long he had it tied in a ponytail. He wore jeans with a hole in the knee and a T-shirt that said CAMP LONE WOLF. Dog tags dangled from a chain around his neck.

"Mr. Jenkins looks worse than ever," Melody whispered. "He should get a haircut."

"He's not as hairy as the hula dancer," Howie pointed out.

Liza didn't listen to her friends. "I'm so excited," she squealed as they jumped out of the van. "I've never been to a luau before."

"Oh, goodie. Now we can dance around like crazy people," Eddie said with a snicker.

Melody punched Eddie in the arm. "You always act like a crazy person so you ought to fit right in."

"I'll go help set up," Eddie's grandmother told them. She went over to the nearby tables and helped Mrs. Jeepers and the parents who were on the luau committee. Beside the tables stood a big white platform decorated with paper flowers. Behind the platform was Lake Erin.

"They decorated the dock. It will look like they're dancing on the water," Melody pointed out.

Liza hopped up and down. "I can't wait to see them dance. Look over there." She pointed. "There's the fire-eater now."

The hairy hula dancer stepped out of the shadows long enough to grab Mr. Jenkins, the camp counselor, by the dog tags.

"Oh, my gosh," Howie gasped. "Do you think they're going to fight?"

"Rats," Eddie complained. "It's too bad Grandma joined this stupid luau committee. She made me leave my water gun at home. I could have blasted them both at once."

"Who's tougher," Melody wondered, "a werewolf or a wolfman?"

"What's the difference?" Liza asked.

Eddie laughed. "A wolfman likes steak for dinner and a werewolf just wants dog food."

"Speaking of dog food," Melody said, "someone is about to get crushed into dog food. They're fighting!"

"I guess that would be a dogfight," Eddie joked.

"This isn't funny," Liza said. "Someone could get hurt."

Melody gasped and Liza whimpered when the two men grabbed each other's arms.

"Wait." Howie shook his head. "They're not fighting. They're hugging."

"Yuck, that's disgusting," Eddie said.

The two men reared their heads back and howled. Then they both licked their lips and looked straight at Eddie.

6

Harry Goto

"Look out," Liza squealed. "They're coming this way. Maybe they plan on eating us for dinner!"

"You're crazy," Eddie told her. "That guy is just a regular old fire-eating dancer. They probably want to say hello."

"Welcome," Mr. Jenkins growled. "I want you to meet my cousin, Harry Goto."

The hairy hula dancer nodded and scratched behind his ear. "Will you watch the dancing?" he growled.

"Yes," Melody said. "We even want to learn how to do it."

Harry smiled a huge smile, showing fanglike teeth. "I'd be happy to show you later when the moon gets full."

Howie gulped. "Is there supposed to be a full moon tonight?"

Mr. Jenkins and Harry looked at each other before both of them threw their heads back and howled with laughter. Then they walked off into the shadows together, still howling.

"We're in big trouble now," Howie moaned. "A full moon is when men turn into werewolves, and I bet it's the same for wolfmen."

Melody looked up at the darkening sky. "I thought the hairy belt made wolfmen come to life."

"There are lots of ways to become a wolfman. I checked at the library," Howie said.

Eddie groaned. "You spend so much time at the library your feet are going to turn into bookends."

Howie ignored Eddie. "You can turn into a wolfman just by drinking water from a wolf's paw print."

"That's disgusting," Liza said.

"According to the book I read, it's true," Howie said. "Of course, there were other ways. But a full moon can't be a good thing for a wolfman."

"It's great for a wolfman," Melody pointed out. "But it's bad luck for kids like us!"

Liza whimpered. "We're all going to be eaten at a wolfman reunion dinner."

Eddie opened his mouth and pretended to chomp on Liza's arm. "Don't worry," he said. "A wolfman would take one bite and spit you out. Too wimpy."

Liza pulled her arm away from Eddie. "At least I'm not rotten like you," she said. "Besides, I am not wimpy, I'm right. Harry Goto is a wolfman and I'll prove it." Without waiting for her friends to follow, Liza stomped off through the woods.

"Where is she going?" Howie asked. "It's almost dark."

"Exactly," Eddie said. "And that means we eat soon. We can't waste our time looking for a make-believe wolfman."

"But Liza could get lost," Howie said.

Melody nodded. "We'd better go after her," she said, "before it's too late."

7

Hungry Hula Dancer

Eddie, Melody, and Howie raced after Liza. They ran past the sign that read DANCERS. They caught up to Liza just as she was trying to peek in the window of a small cabin. Unfortunately, she was too short to see in.

"I think he's in here," Liza whispered.

"You'd have to be a giant to look into those windows," Eddie complained.

"Let me stand on your back," Melody told Eddie.

Eddie shook his head. "No, we tried that before and I almost got killed. Besides, do I look like a ladder to you?"

"No," Melody giggled, "you look like a sawhorse. Now bend down." Melody scrambled up Eddie's back and held on to the wall to keep from falling. Slowly,

33

she edged her face up to the window. She looked in for a second before jumping down.

"Is there a wolfman inside?" Liza asked.

"No," Melody told her, "just a bunch of ladies in grass skirts and flower necklaces."

"Those are called leis," Howie pointed out.

"I don't care if they're called boa constrictors," Eddie said. "Let's get back to the dinner. I'm getting hungry."

Howie checked his glow-in-the-dark watch. "We have a few minutes before it's time to eat."

Liza squealed. "Did you hear that?"

The hair on each kid's neck stood up as they heard a low growling. "I think it's coming from over there," Liza said nervously, pointing to a nearby small log building.

"That doesn't look like a regular cabin," Melody said. "It looks like a doghouse."

"What could be making that noise?" Howie whispered.

"There's only one way to find out," Eddie said, hurrying over to the building with his friends close behind.

"Maybe we should go back to the dinner instead," Liza whispered, grabbing Eddie's arm before he got too close to the small building.

Eddie shook his head. "This was your idea," he pointed out. "We've come this far, we might as well see what's inside."

"There are no windows in this cabin," Howie said.

"Then I'll have to look in the door," Eddie said bravely. Slowly, he tiptoed up to the wooden door, grabbed the rusty handle, and pulled. They couldn't see inside, but they could definitely hear.

"Grrrr. Grrrr. GRRR!"

Everyone held their breaths while Eddie peeked inside. After one look, Eddie raced away from the cabin. Liza, Melody, and Howie ran after him as fast as they

could. They flew into the woods. Vines grabbed at their sneakers and strange noises echoed all around them. They ran and ran until Liza couldn't run anymore. She dropped to the ground and panted. "Go on," Liza gasped. "Leave me here and save yourselves."

"Save ourselves from what?" Eddie asked.

"The wolfman!" Melody snapped. "Why else would we be running?"

"What wolfman?" Eddie asked innocently.

"The wolfman inside the shack, you dope," Howie said.

Eddie grinned. "There wasn't anything in that cabin except a hungry hula dancer with a growling stomach."

"Then why did you run?" Liza asked.

"Because," Eddie said, "you've been doing nothing except telling silly wolfman stories. I thought it was time for some exercise."

Melody held her fist against Eddie's cheek. "I ought to clobber you for scaring us about nothing."

Howie interrupted Melody. "You mean you didn't see anything strange in that cabin?"

"Well," Eddie said slowly. "I did notice that Harry was combing that furry belt with his long fingernails. It was disgusting. Hasn't he ever heard of nail clippers?"

"We were lucky," Liza told them.

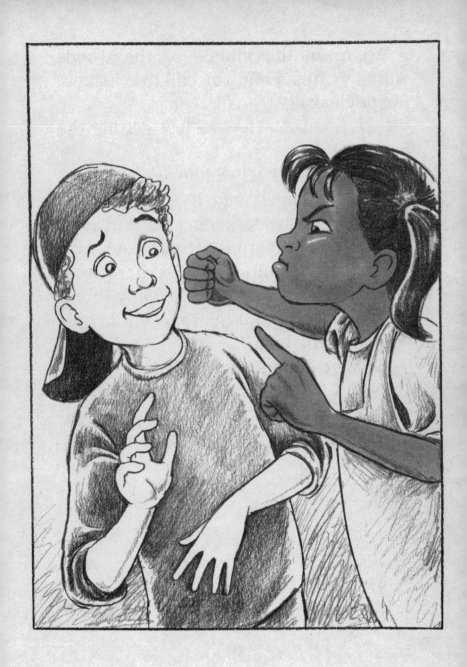

"We're in the middle of the woods with a wolfman and you call that lucky?" Melody asked.

Liza nodded. "He was just getting the belt ready."

"Ready for what?" Eddie asked.

Liza shuddered and looked over her shoulder into the darkening woods. Crickets chirped all around them and Liza swatted a mosquito away from her cheek. "Harry was getting the belt ready to put on tonight when all the innocent people will be at the luau."

"So he can dance for us," Melody said.

"No," Liza said seriously. "So he can turn into a vicious, hairy, and very hungry wolfman."

8

Fur Ball

"I think you're just one big fur ball," Eddie complained. "I'm tired of all this crazy wolfman talk." Eddie turned away from his friends and followed the path back to the luau.

Silently, Liza, Melody, and Howie followed Eddie. They ended up back at the beach, where the tables were already decorated with tiny candles. Lanterns hung from nearby trees and the big paper flowers the kids had made were strewn throughout the trees. A big pit was loaded with wood and ready for a fire. A brown-haired third-grader named Jake was tossing a coconut to his friends Ryan and Daniel while the other kids were busy talking near the big fire pit.

"I think it's almost time for the dancers

41

to start," Liza said, pointing to two danc- ers setting up the big drums.

Howie pulled his friends away from the tables. "Maybe we should play it safe, just in case Harry is a wolfman."

"But what can we do?" Liza asked. "No one would believe us if we told them." She looked at Principal Davis and their teacher, Mrs. Jeepers. They were stand- ing with a group of parents drinking from coconut cups.

Howie pointed to one of the lanterns. "The book said that the belt only worked in darkness, so we have to make sure there's plenty of light for the luau."

"These little lanterns aren't going to give off much light when it gets really dark," Liza agreed.

"I guess it wouldn't hurt to have more light. If Liza's right, then Harry can't turn into a wolfman," Melody said.

"If Liza's wrong . . ." Howie said.

"Which she is," Eddie interrupted.

Howie kept on talking. "Even if she is

wrong, then the worst thing that could happen is that there's plenty of light for the luau."

"I like daylight better than pitch-black darkness, anyway," Liza said.

Eddie swatted at one of the paper flowers hanging in a tree. "What difference does it make?" he asked. "There's no way we can turn the night into day."

"How do you know until we try?" Melody asked.

"That's right," Liza said. "We can do anything if we put our minds to it."

"That's the spirit," Howie said. "There's bound to be some flashlights around here somewhere."

"And some candles," Liza suggested.

"How about a neon sign that's flashing MY FRIENDS ARE NUTS?" Eddie asked. "I'm sure they have two or three of those lying around somewhere."

Melody put her hands on her hips and stared Eddie in the face. "If you aren't part of the solution, you're part of the problem."

"That's right," Liza said.

"Did you make that up?" Howie asked.

Melody shook her head. "No, it's something I heard my mom say. I think someone famous said it once."

"I don't care if the president himself said it," Eddie muttered. "You guys are still fighting a losing battle."

"Well, I am prepared to fight," Liza said. "Are you?"

9

Wild Wolfman Chase

"I'm ready to make you stop talking nonsense," Eddie said. "And if it means going on a wild wolfman chase, then I'll do it."

"Here's what we have to do," Howie said, pulling his friends close.

"It will never work," Eddie told his friends when Howie finished talking.

"We have to try," Liza said. "It may mean the difference between having the barbecue and BEING the barbecue!"

"Stop it," Eddie said. "You're making me hungrier!"

The four friends slipped into the shadows of the towering hemlock trees and made their way back up the trail to the cabins. "I'll check out Cabin Silver Wolf," Howie said.

"I'll try that storage shack over there," Eddie said.

"I'll search Cabin Gray Wolf and Liza can take Cabin Red Wolf," Melody suggested.

"But I don't want to be by myself," Liza said. "Something might sneak up and get me."

"We have to split up," Howie said, "or we'll run out of time."

"If we waste too much time," Eddie added as his stomach rumbled, "there won't be a single morsel of food left for us."

"If Liza's right and we get back after the sun goes down," Melody said, "being hungry will be the least of our troubles."

"I know I'm right," Liza said with a deep breath. "We'll split up and meet back at the luau as fast as we can."

Without another word, the four friends went their separate ways to search for the only thing they knew could save them. By the time they met back at the luau, the sun was beginning to sink below the horizon. The rest of the kids were gathered around the fire and the beautiful dancers wearing grass skirts were climbing onto the platform to perform.

Liza was the first one to make it back to the luau. She hid behind a tree and waited for her friends. When Melody hurried to the clearing, Liza pulled her friend into the shadows.

Howie joined them carrying two lanterns. "These should be bright enough," Howie said. But when he clicked on the switches, nothing happened.

"The batteries must be dead," Liza said. "Try this."

Howie took a flashlight from Liza and held the light under his chin. The dim beam held only enough light to make Howie's face glow like something from one of Liza's worst nightmares.

"All I found were these candles," Melody said. "But I didn't see any matches."

"Eddie was right," Liza said sadly. "This isn't enough to light up the luau, and it's definitely not enough to melt the magic from Harry's belt."

"Where is Eddie, anyway?" Melody asked.

"I haven't seen him," Howie said. "I'm more worried about where Harry is."

"There," Liza said, pointing to the deep shadows near the edge of the clearing. Harry stood watching the kids who were

gathered around the bonfire. "As soon as the sun sets we'll be wolfman burgers," Liza said sadly.

"We may have a little time," Howie told her. "He's not wearing the fur belt yet."

Howie was right. The thick brown-and-black belt was hanging from a branch near the platform where the other dancers had gathered.

"I wonder why he's just watching," Liza said with a shiver.

"I bet he's trying to decide which kid to save for dessert," Melody said.

"Not if I have anything to do with it!" Eddie said from behind them.

"Eddie!" Liza shrieked. "Where have you been?"

Eddie stood up tall and puffed out his chest. "I have been doing what I do best," he said smugly. "I've been planning to save the day."

"And how are you going to do that?" Melody asked.

"With these!" Eddie said, holding out a bulging bag.

Liza, Melody, and Howie peered inside the bag. "Are you crazy?" Liza yelled. "Those twinkling lights are only good for decorating Christmas trees."

"What's wrong?" Eddie asked. "You said to get lights and I did. I found all of these in the storage shed. You should be thanking me."

"Don't you know anything?" Liza argued. "Those lights aren't bright enough."

"They're brighter than your brain," Eddie told her.

Howie stepped between his friends. "We have to work together. This is no time for fighting."

Just then, one of the drummers started beating a slow rhythm on the giant drum. "Howie's right," Melody said as she reached into the bag and pulled out a string of lights. "We have to hurry."

The four kids raced around the edges of the clearing, draping Christmas tree

lights on all the low branches. The final rays of the sun were disappearing as the kids draped the last string of Christmas lights on a scraggly bush. Eddie pulled a long extension cord out of his bag. "Once I plug this in," Eddie said, "our wolfman worries will vanish."

Eddie was right about one thing. The wolfman did vanish. So did everything else, because when Eddie plugged in the extension cord every light at the luau went out. A strong breeze whipped through the camp and all the candles blew out, too. It was pitch-black.

10

Wolfman's Supermarket

"You've blown a fuse!" Howie yelled. Melody gasped and Liza screamed, but Eddie took off running. When he did, he tripped over the extension cord and fell right into Melody. Melody crashed into Liza and they all landed in a big heap.

The only light came from the huge luau bonfire casting strange shadows around the clearing, but it was enough for Liza to see all the panicked people. Kids screamed, teachers yelled, and parents hollered. Jake threw a coconut in the air and it came straight down on Principal Davis's bald head. The dancers in grass skirts bumped into one another on the platform and somebody knocked over the drums.

The only person who didn't seem upset

was Mr. Jenkins. Liza noticed that he slipped quietly from the clearing and disappeared up the trail. "I think Mr. Jenkins just went for the salt and pepper," Liza whispered.

"This is terrible," Melody told her friends as they untangled their arms and legs. "Instead of saving everybody, we've turned this luau into a wolfman's supermarket. All Harry Goto has to do is go to the nearest kid and gobble him up."

"There's so much noise, we can't even yell out a warning," Liza added.

"We're dog food, and there's nothing we can do about it," Melody said.

"There's still one thing that can save us," Howie said as he helped his friends up. "We have to get that belt away from Harry."

"Howie is right," Liza said. "If we can keep Harry from putting on that belt, we'll all be safe."

"Then we have to hurry," Melody said, "because Harry looks like he just heard a dinner bell."

Liza, Howie, and Eddie looked in the direction Melody pointed. Sure enough, Harry was making his way around the frantic kids, parents, and teachers. And he was heading straight for his fur belt.

"This way is fastest!" Howie hollered.

"No, this way," Melody said.

When Melody and Howie took off running, they ran right into each other and landed on the ground again.

"Oh, for Pete's sake," Eddie grumbled. "Must I do everything?" Eddie didn't wait for an answer. He jumped over his friends, sprinted around two parents, and raced straight for Harry's magic belt.

Liza helped Melody and Howie scramble up from the ground, and then they all ran after their friend.

Eddie hopped up on the dance platform with Harry hot on his heels.

Together, Harry and Eddie reached the branch where the fur belt dangled. Harry reached for it, but Eddie was faster. He snatched the belt and backed away from the hairy hula dancer.

"We're saved!" Liza yelped.

But then, Eddie did the unthinkable.

"STOP!" Melody, Liza, and Howie screamed together.

It was too late. Liza, Melody, and Howie watched in horror as Eddie wrapped the magic fur belt around his own waist.

11

Dance, Dance, Dance

A huge spotlight clicked on and flooded the stage with light. Eddie stood right in the center of the light with the hairy belt on. He put his arm over his face to keep from being blinded by the light.

"Mr. Jenkins must have replaced the fuse," Melody said.

Liza shuddered. "He was just in time. The light is bright enough to stop the magic of the belt."

"What was Eddie thinking when he put on that belt?" Melody asked. "He might have turned into a wolfman! Is he crazy?"

Howie nodded and pointed to the stage. "Yes, I think he is."

Parents and teachers laughed at Eddie standing dead center on the stage. Jake and his friends started chanting, "Dance, dance, DANCE!"

Eddie squinted at the crowd. He saw Harry backing away from the bright light. Then the whole crowd starting cheering for Eddie. "Dance, dance, dance!"

Some female hula dancers came beside Eddie and danced. One of them tied a grass skirt around Eddie's waist, completely covering the furry belt. The drummers started beating out a rhythm. Eddie shrugged and did the only thing he could think of. He started dancing.

Only Eddie didn't sway his hips gently or move his hands slowly like the other dancers. Eddie waved his hands wildly over his head and jumped in crazy circles. The crowd clapped their hands and stomped their feet to the drum's rhythm.

Liza giggled. "Eddie is a dancing fool."

"I never knew he had it in him," Howie said as a pretty hula dancer waved her hands all around Eddie.

Melody rolled her eyes. "You never know what Eddie will do next."

"I just hope that spotlight doesn't go out," Howie said with a worried look on his face. "That belt could still turn Eddie into a hairy wolfman."

Liza gulped. "What are we going to do?" she asked. "That dance can't last forever." Liza was right. The drummers were already slowing the song down and only a few dancers remained onstage.

"We can't let the dance stop," Melody squealed. "Mr. Jenkins might turn off the spotlight."

Howie shrugged. "There's nothing we can do."

"Oh, yes there is," Melody said. She grabbed a grass skirt from the pile by the platform, tied it around her waist, and jumped onstage. She started her own version of the hula dance, shaking her hips and waving her hands around.

Liza and Howie looked at each other and did what they had to do. They both grabbed grass skirts and jumped on the stage. When the drums slowed their rhythms, Melody and Howie would start dancing faster and faster until the drummers caught up with them. Liza could see their principal, Mr. Davis, frowning, but she didn't stop dancing.

Melody was sure their dancing would come to a screeching halt when Mrs. Jeepers' hand rested on her brooch. But then, Mrs. Jeepers smiled her odd little half smile. She grabbed a grass skirt, climbed on the stage, and started dancing, too. The parents cheered, grabbed paper flowers to stick in their hair, and started dancing around the bonfire.

Principal Davis scratched his bald head and looked at the parents, the kids, and Mrs. Jeepers as they twirled and swayed to the pounding rhythms of the drums. Then the Bailey School principal grinned, grabbed a grass skirt, and started dancing, too.

Everybody was dancing. Everyone, that

is, except Harry. He stayed in the shadows and out of the bright spotlight, watching Eddie.

Howie, Melody, and Liza twirled around on the stage. Eddie didn't twirl. He was so busy hopping, jumping, and twisting that he didn't notice how close he was to the edge of the platform. But Harry noticed.

"No!" Harry screamed from the shadows, only he was too late. Eddie teetered on the edge of the dock. He waved his hands in the air, trying to keep his balance. But it was no use. Eddie slipped off the edge of the stage and disappeared into the dark water. The music stopped and everyone gasped. Then someone jumped into the lake. Howie, Melody, and Liza screamed when they realized it was Harry who dived into the water after Eddie.

12

Drowning Poodle

"I can't see anything," Melody said, peering into the dark waters of Lake Erin.

"This is all my fault," Liza moaned. "I'll never forgive myself if Eddie drowns."

"I just hope he didn't turn into a wolf-man's sandwich," Howie said softly as parents, teachers, and students rushed onto the stage to see if Eddie was okay.

"There he is," Liza said with relief. Harry and Eddie pulled themselves onto the dock. They were both soaking wet, but neither one looked hurt.

Melody giggled, "Eddie looks like a drowned poodle."

Howie grabbed Melody's shoulder. "Look at Harry. Something is very strange about him."

"Of course he's strange," Melody whispered. "He's a wolfman."

Howie shook his head. "No, look." Melody, Liza, and Howie stared at the wet Harry. His hair was slicked back off his face, and he didn't look nearly as hairy.

"What happened to his hair?" Liza gasped. "It's disappearing."

"It just looks that way," Melody pointed out, "because he's wet."

"Maybe," Howie said, pulling Eddie away from the crowd of people. "Or it could be our wolfman troubles are over, thanks to Eddie."

"What did I do?" Eddie asked.

"You fell into the water," Howie told him. "And the water broke the wolfman spell on the hairy belt."

Liza patted Eddie on the back. "I guess that means Eddie is a hero."

Melody extended her arms and danced around Eddie, waving a flower in the air. "What in the world are you doing now?" Liza asked Melody.

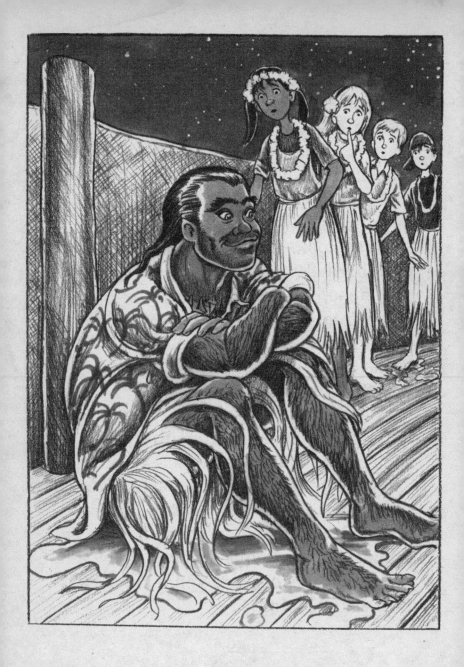

Melody grinned and sang her answer. "I'm dancing the hula story of the fierce wolfman warrior — Eddie! It will be the perfect performance to go along with my Hawaii report on Monday."

Eddie groaned. "I shouldn't have to do a report," he said. "After all, I was too busy battling a wolfman!"

"There's only one way you could get out of doing your report for Mrs. Jeepers," Melody told him, "and that's by turning into a wolfman in front of the whole class!"

Liza and Howie laughed. Then they joined Melody and danced around the dripping wet Eddie.

There was only one thing left for Eddie to do. He shrugged, patted the wolfman belt, then leaned his head back and howled.

Debbie Dadey and Marcia Thornton Jones have fun writing stories together. When they both worked at an elementary school in Lexington, Kentucky, Debbie was the school librarian and Marcia was a teacher. During their lunch break in the school cafeteria, they came up with the idea of the Bailey School kids.

Recently Debbie and her family moved to Aurora, Illinois. Marcia and her husband still live in Kentucky where she continues to teach. How do these authors still write together? They talk on the phone and use computers and fax machines!

THE BAILEY CITY

by Marcia Thornton Jones
and Debbie Dadey

MONSTERS

Check out who's visiting the Hauntly Manor Inn!

Annie is tired of studying for the big spelling bee. She wishes she could just spell every word without even trying. So, Kilmer's Great-uncle Nilrem casts a spell to make her wish come true!

Now Annie is worried. She doesn't want to cheat. What's worse, Issy has overheard the whole thing—and she wants to report Great-uncle Nilrem to the police!

#6: Spooky Spells

Coming to bookstores in May!

BCMT1098

Under the stairs, a magical world awaits you!

THE SECRETS OF DROON

A New Series by Tony Abbott

The world of Droon is a magical and beautiful place. But it's a place where all is not well.

Eric and his friends have stumbled upon the door to Droon. And now it's too late to turn back!

Look for

The Secrets of Droon:

#1: *The Hidden Stairs and the Magic Carpet*

#2: *The Fire Palace and the Enchanted Pool*

Coming to bookstores everywhere in May!

■ SCHOLASTIC

SD1098